# Dear Parent:

Congratulations! Your child is taking the first steps on an exciting journey. The destination? Independent reading!

**STEP INTO READING®** will help your child get there. The program offers five steps to reading success. Each step includes fun stories and colorful art. There are also Step into Reading Sticker Books, Step into Reading Math Readers, Step into Reading Phonics Readers, Step into Reading Write-In Readers, and Step into Reading Phonics Boxed Sets—a complete literacy program with something to interest every child.

## Learning to Read, Step by Step!

**Ready to Read** **Preschool–Kindergarten**

**• big type and easy words • rhyme and rhythm • picture clues**

For children who know the alphabet and are eager to begin reading.

**Reading with Help** **Preschool–Grade 1**

**• basic vocabulary • short sentences • simple stories**

For children who recognize familiar words and sound out new words with help.

**Reading on Your Own** **Grades 1–3**

**• engaging characters • easy-to-follow plots • popular topics**

For children who are ready to read on their own.

**Reading Paragraphs** **Grades 2–3**

**• challenging vocabulary • short paragraphs • exciting stories**

For newly independent readers who read simple sentences with confidence.

**Ready for Chapters** **Grades 2–4**

**• chapters • longer paragraphs • full-color art**

For children who want to take the plunge into chapter books but still like colorful pictures.

**STEP INTO READING®** is designed to give every child a successful reading experience. The grade levels are only guides. Children can progress through the steps at their own speed, developing confidence in their reading, no matter what their grade.

Remember, a lifetime love of reading starts with a single step!

# FIVE TOY TALES

Copyright © 2012 Disney/Pixar. All rights reserved. Slinky® Dog is a registered trademark of Poof-Slinky, Inc. © Poof-Slinky, Inc. Mr. and Mrs. Potato Head® and Tinkertoy® are registered trademarks of Hasbro, Inc. Used with permission. © Hasbro, Inc. All rights reserved. Mattel toys used with permission. © Mattel Inc. All rights reserved. Etch A Sketch® © The Ohio Art Company. Toddle Tots® by Little Tikes®. Published in the United States by Random House Children's Books, a division of Random House, Inc., 1745 Broadway, New York, NY 10019, and in Canada by Random House of Canada Limited, Toronto, in conjunction with Disney Enterprises, Inc.

The works in this collection were originally published separately in the United States as *Friends Forever*, copyright © 2009 Disney Enterprises, Inc./Pixar; *Toy to Toy*, copyright © 2010 Disney/Pixar; *The Great Toy Escape*, copyright © 2010 Disney/Pixar; *Move Out!*, copyright © 2011 Disney/Pixar; and *A Spooky Adventure*, copyright © 2011 Disney/Pixar.

Step into Reading, Random House, and the Random House colophon are registered trademarks of Random House, Inc.

Visit us on the Web!
StepIntoReading.com
www.randomhouse.com/kids

Educators and librarians, for a variety of teaching tools, visit us at
www.randomhouse.com/teachers

ISBN: 978-0-7364-2845-3

MANUFACTURED IN CHINA 10 9 8 7 6 5 4 3 2 1

STEP INTO READING®

Step 1 and 2 Books

A Collection of Five Early Readers

Random House New York

# CONTENTS

STEP INTO READING®

Disney · PIXAR

# FRIENDS FOREVER

By Melissa Lagonegro

Illustrated by Studio IBOIX
and the Disney Storybook Artists

Random House New York

TRIPLE·R

Buzz and Woody are
Andy's favorite toys.
They are
best friends.

Oh, no!

Woody has been stolen!

Woody is trapped.
He meets Jessie,
Bullseye, and
the Prospector.

They are
the Roundup gang.
Woody is a member of
the Roundup gang, too!

Buzz wants
to save Woody.
Andy's other toys help.

Woody learns about
the Roundup gang.
He makes friends.
He has fun.

Buzz looks for Woody.

Andy's other toys help.

Woody misses Andy.
But he will not leave
his new friends.
He is worried about them.

Buzz finds Woody!
He wants Woody
to come home.
So do the other toys.

Woody asks
the Roundup gang
to come home
with him!
But the Prospector
blocks their way.

He will not let

the others leave.

He is not their friend

after all.

Woody and
the Roundup gang
are in trouble.

The man is taking them
far away.
Buzz and Slinky
try to help.

The toys go after Woody!

Buzz drives a truck.

Buzz has a plan
to save Woody.
The toys follow Woody.
They go to the airport.

Buzz races
to the rescue!

Oh, no!
Jessie is trapped
in the case.
She is put
on a plane!

Woody tries
to help Jessie.
They are in danger!

Buzz and Bullseye
save Jessie and Woody!

The toys go
home to Andy.
They will all be
friends forever.

STEP INTO READING®

# Toy to Toy

By Tennant Redbank

Illustrated by
Caroline LaVelle Egan, Adrienne Brown,
Scott Tilley, and Studio IBOIX

Random House New York

These are Andy's toys.

LIGHTYEAR

Woody is a cowboy.
He wears a cowboy hat.

Buzz is a spaceman and Woody's best friend.

Slinky is a dog.

He can stretch!

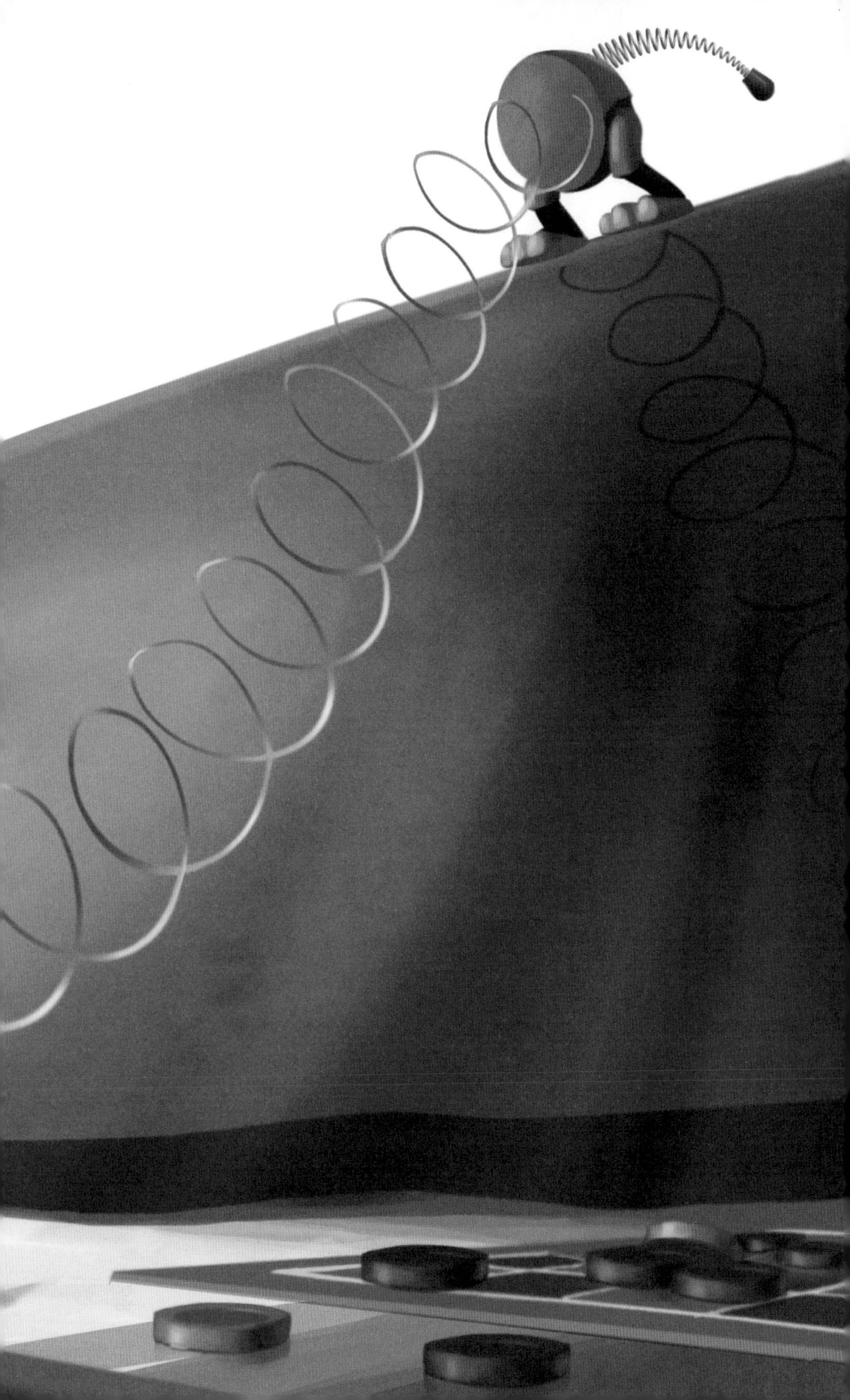

Yee-haw!
Jessie is a cowgirl.
She likes
to ride Bullseye.

Hamm is a piggy bank.

He holds pennies.

These toys are green.
They stick together.

Roar!

Rex is a dinosaur.

Andy is big now.

Andy's toys get

a new home.

They meet new toys!

Lotso is a teddy bear.

He is the boss.

Lotso likes to hug!

Big Baby is
the biggest toy.

Chunk has two faces.

Sparks spits

real sparks.

Twitch looks like
a big bad bug.

Stretch is made
of rubber.

All the toys
are ready to play!

Will Andy's toys like their new home?

STEP INTO READING®

# The Great Toy Escape

By Kitty Richards

Illustrated by Caroline LaVelle Egan, Adrienne Brown,
Scott Tilley, and Studio IBOIX

Random House New York

Andy's toys love
to play.
But Andy is grown up.
He does not play
with his toys
anymore.

The toys must find
a new home.
They climb
into a car.

The car goes
to Sunnyside Daycare.

Sunnyside is full
of toys!

A bear named Lotso is

in charge.

There are kids
at Sunnyside every day.
Andy's toys are happy.
The kids will play
with them!

But Woody is not happy.

He misses Andy.

He leaves.

It is time to play!

The little kids pull.

They throw.

They yell.

The toys do not like it.

The toys want

to go home.

But the door is locked!

Lotso is mean.
He will not let
Andy's toys leave.

Lotso and his gang lock up Andy's toys!

Then Woody comes back.
He has a plan.
They will escape!

That night,
Woody and Slinky
steal the key!

The toys sneak outside.
They do not
make a sound.

The toys try to escape.
Oh, no!
They fall
into a garbage truck.

The truck goes
to the dump.
The toys are
in danger!
They must escape.

They run!
Woody tells them
to hurry.
They look
for a way out.

They slide!
The toys hold hands
to stay together.

At last,
they escape!

The toys hide
in the garbage.
They go back
to Andy's house.

The toys are safe.
They are happy
to be home.

Andy finds his toys
a new owner.
She loves to play!
And the toys love
their new home.

STEP INTO READING® STEP 2

# MOVE OUT!

Adapted by Apple Jordan

Based on an original story by Jason Katz

Illustrated by Allan Batson and
the Disney Storybook Artists

Random House New York

Andy is grown up.
He does not play
with his toys anymore.

The Green Army Men
have a plan.
Sarge tells his troops
to move out!
They salute Woody
and Buzz.

Then the troops jump
out the window.
They soar into the air.

They will find
a new home.

The troops land
at a toy store.
Sarge looks for a child
to take them home.

SAL'S
TOY BARN
UNDER NEW
MANAGEMENT

Inside the store,

Sarge sees a boy.

The troops hide
in the boy's bag.
They will go home
with him!

But the boy
does not go home.
He goes
to a bakery.

The boy drops his bag.
The troops fall
on the floor.
They look around.

A baker sees the troops.
He puts them
on a birthday cake.

He puts the cake

in the freezer.

The troops are cold!

The next day,
the cake goes
to a birthday party.

Sarge sees a boy.
Sarge has a plan!
The troops will
go home
with the boy.

Sarge watches the boy.
The troops wait.
The boy leaves
Pizza Planet.

The troops run
after the boy.
But he is too fast.
They cannot catch up.

Sarge spots
a pizza truck.
The truck can catch up
to the boy!

Sargé gives an order.
The troops jump
on board.

The truck speeds away
with the troops.
But it is windy
on the truck.

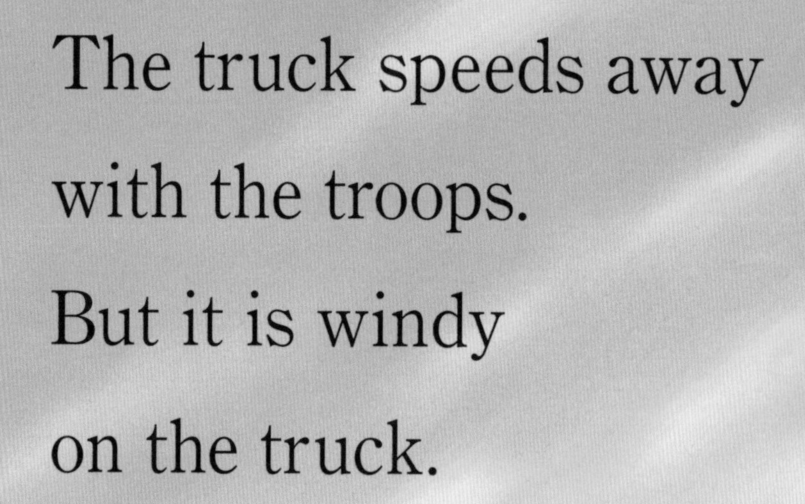

The troops
are blown
into the air!

The troops land
at a gas station.

They set up camp
for the night.

The next morning,
Sarge hears a loud noise.
He is lifted
into a garbage can!

Then Sarge is tossed
into a garbage truck.
The truck drives away.

Sarge's troops
will rescue him!
They make a chain.
They reach for Sarge.
Sarge is safe!

Sarge and the troops
jump off the truck.
They land
by a playground.

The troops meet
a group of toys.
They are
at Sunnyside Daycare.

There are kids
at Sunnyside.
At last, the troops
have a new home!

STEP INTO READING®

# A Spooky Adventure

By Apple Jordan

Illustrated by Alan Batson
and Lori Tyminski

Random House New York

Woody and his friends
loved their new home.
Bonnie loved to play
with her new toys.

Bonnie's favorite game
was Bakery.
But her bakery
was spooky!

One rainy day,
Bonnie and her family
went out.
Her toys were home alone.

Outside,
thunder boomed.
Lightning flashed
in the sky.

The Potato Heads jumped.

Bullseye hid in a drawer.

Slinky peeked
out the window.
Rex said the house
was haunted!

Jessie hugged Bullseye.
Buzz turned
on his laser light.
Woody said the house
was not haunted.

Bonnie's old toys would show their new friends.

Rex looked
under Bonnie's bed.
He saw monsters!

But Trixie said
there were no monsters.
She crawled
under the bed.

Trixie showed Rex
the monsters.
They were
Bonnie's bunny slippers!

The toys
heard scratching
at the window.
Bullseye hid
behind Woody.
Was it a ghost?

Buttercup opened the curtain.

It was not a ghost!
Bonnie's kite was stuck
in the tree.

Soon the toys

heard a spooky sound.

Hooo! Hooo! Hooo!

Hamm said it
was a goblin.

Buzz and Woody
led the gang
down the hall.

Mr. Pricklepants
opened the blinds.
The sound was
not a goblin.
It was just an owl!

Thud!
The toys heard a sound
from the kitchen.

The toys went
to the kitchen.
Would they see
a scary creature?

Chuckles told them
to watch out.
But Woody was
not worried.

Chuckles opened
the closet door.
Woody froze.
Buzz jumped.
Rex yelled.

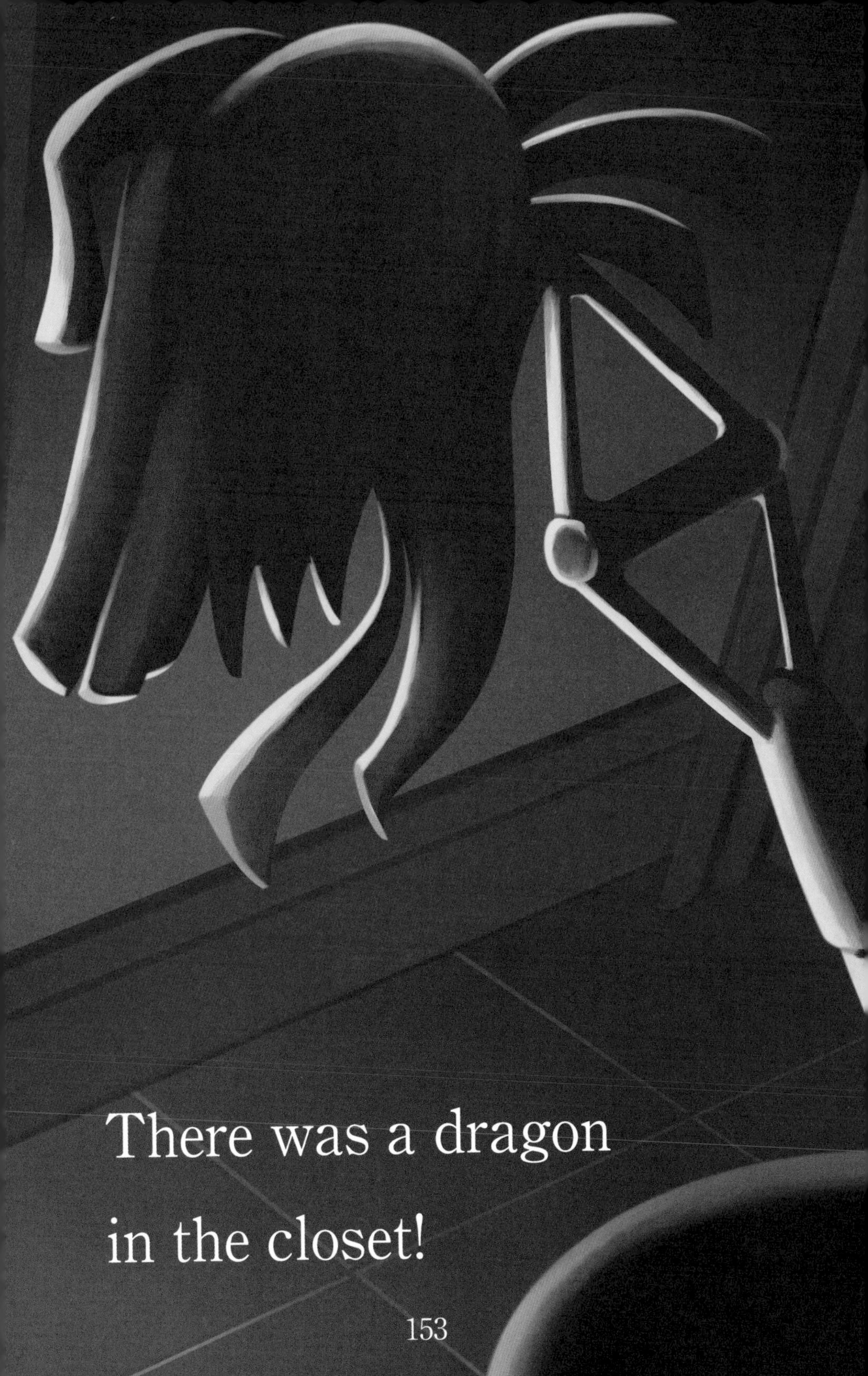

There was a dragon
in the closet!

Chuckles turned on the light.

It was not a dragon!

It was just an old mop.

The toys all laughed.
There were no monsters.
There were no ghosts.
There were no goblins.
There were no dragons.
Bonnie's house
was not haunted.

But sometimes it was still a little spooky.